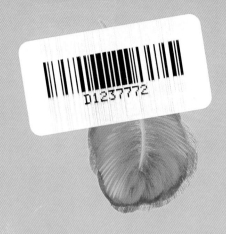

By a Blazing Blue Sea

WRITTEN BY S. T. GARNE

ILLUSTRATED BY LORI LOHSTOETER

GULLIVER BOOKS
HARCOURT BRACE & COMPANY
San Diego   New York   London

Library of Congress Cataloging-in-Publication Data
Garne, S. T.
By a blazing blue sea/S. T. Garne; illustrated by Lori Lohstoeter.
p.   cm.
"Gulliver Books."
Summary: A rhyming description of the simple and colorful life of a Caribbean fisherman.
ISBN 0-15-201780-1
[1. Color—Fiction. 2. Caribbean Area—Fiction. 3. Stories in rhyme.] I. Lohstoeter, Lori, ill. II. Title.
PZ8.3.G1866By   1999
[E]—DC21   97-37644

First edition
A C E F D B

Printed in Singapore

The illustrations in this book were done in acrylics on illustration board.
The display type was set in Pabst Langston.
The text type was set in Stone Informal.
Color separations by United Graphic Pte. Ltd., Singapore
Printed and bound by Tien Wah Press, Singapore
This book was printed on totally chlorine-free Nymolla Matte Art paper.
Production supervision by Stanley Redfern and Pascha Gerlinger
Designed by Judythe Sieck

For R. K. Murray and his grandson Jack
—S. T. G.

For two sweet new souls on this earth—
John Douglas and Mitchell Harrison, my nephews
—L. L.

Below sweeping green hills
On a crescent of land,
Between craggy black rocks
Lies a white strip of sand.

And there on the beach
By a blazing blue sea
Stands the twisted gray trunk
Of an old kapok tree.

Beneath this great tree
Where the rambling roots spread,
Lives a wrinkled old man
In a small orange shed.

He has a cot in the corner
With a soft yellow sheet,
A sturdy wood table,
And one purple seat.

In the pink dawn he fishes,
In the blue noon he sleeps
'Neath a leafy green awning
Where dappled sun seeps.

When the soft shadows lengthen
He sews his red sails
And patches his roof
With rust-covered nails.

In the black night he sleeps—
Heavy breath, tired bones.
It's still dark when he rises,
Bare feet on sharp stones.

Some think the old man
Is a poor simple fool—
No power, no money,
No people to rule.

But when the silver moon pales
And the black night is gone,
Content the man smiles
In a rose-colored dawn.